For Ethan and Nicholas, and Jasper
and Jensen —YP

For our beautiful new daughter Zoe
and her big sister Jade x —DM

Scholastic Australia
345 Pacific Highway Lindfield NSW 2070
An imprint of Scholastic Australia Pty Limited
PO Box 579 Gosford NSW 2250
ABN 11 000 614 577
www.scholastic.com.au

Part of the Scholastic Group
Sydney · Auckland · New York · Toronto · London · Mexico City
· New Delhi · Hong Kong · Buenos Aires · Puerto Rico

Published by Scholastic Australia in 2013.
Text and illustrations copyright © Scholastic Australia, 2013.
Text by Yvette Poshoglian.
Cover design, illustrations and inside illustrations by Danielle McDonald.

All rights reserved. No part of this publication may be reproduced or transmitted
in any form or by any means, electronic or mechanical, including photocopying,
recording, storage in an information retrieval system, or otherwise, without the prior
written permission of the publisher, unless specifically permitted under the Australian
Copyright Act 1968 as amended.

National Library of Australia Cataloguing-in-Publication entry

Author: Poshoglian, Yvette.
Title: The Christmas Surprise / by Yvette Poshoglian, illustrated by Danielle McDonald.
ISBN: 9781742839219 (pbk.)
Series: Poshoglian, Yvette. Ella and Olivia; 9.
Target Audience: For primary school age.
Subjects: Christmas Stories.
Other Authors/Contributors: McDonald, Danielle.

Dewey Number: A823.4

Typeset in Buccardi.

Printed by McPherson's Printing Group, Maryborough, VIC.

Scholastic Australia's policy, in association with McPherson's Printing Group, is to use
papers that are renewable and made efficiently from wood grown in responsibly managed
forest, so as to minimise its environmental footprint.

10 9 8 7 6 5   15 16 17 / 1

MIX
Paper from
responsible sources
FSC® C001695

eLLa AND Olivia

The Christmas Surprise

By
Yvette Poshoglian

Illustrated by
Danielle McDonald

A Scholastic Australia Book

Chapter One

Ella and Olivia are sisters. Ella is seven years old. Olivia is five-and-a-half years old. Ella and Olivia both love to dance and play netball.

Their little brother Max is nearly two years old. Bob is their golden retriever. He is still a puppy and loves getting into mischief.

It's tinsel time! Ella and Olivia are counting down to their favourite time of the year—Christmas!

Nanna's Christmas pudding, candy canes, stockings and lots of surprises are just around the corner. Mr Jones, the grocer, has already hung Christmas decorations in his shop window.

'I can't wait for Christmas Day,' says Ella. She loves getting presents!
'Santa only visits good children,' says Mum.
'We are angels, Mum!' says Olivia. Mum always calls them her 'little angels'.
'Gurgle,' says Max.

Bob wags his tail. Bob can always sniff excitement in the air.

Crash! Dad and Uncle Stu struggle with the Christmas tree.

'It's a big fella this year,' says Uncle Stu. 'I hope it fits.' When they stand the tree up, the top branches touch the ceiling. It is huge!

'The prickles are dropping everywhere!' says Olivia. She picks up the pine needles from the tree that have scattered on the floor.

Real Christmas trees are pine trees. They have a fresh, strong smell that tingles your nose.
'It's beginning to smell a lot like Christmas,' says Dad. He wipes his brow. 'Phew! That was a heavy one!'

Mum brings out the boxes
holding all the Christmas
decorations.

'Are you girls going to help?'
she asks. Ella and Olivia
can't wait to decorate the
tree. The sooner the tree is
ready, the sooner Christmas
will come!

Mum slowly unwraps the
precious decorations. Ella
and Olivia are allowed to
hang some.

They are very careful. Ella
puts up a glass stocking.
Olivia puts up a glass sleigh.
'They're so beautiful,' Olivia
says, twirling the sleigh so it
catches the light.

There are so many decorations to put up. It takes all afternoon! There are paper decorations that Ella made when she was very little. Olivia made some this year at school. There are even some decorations that Dad made when he was a kid. They are very old now. Soon there is only one decoration lying in the box to be put up.

'Whose turn is it to put the star on the top of the tree this year?' asks Dad.

'Mine?' asks Uncle Stu, hopefully.

'Don't be silly,' says Olivia. 'It's MY turn!'

'No, it's MY turn!' cries Ella.

Both girls reach for the decoration at the same time and PULL. The beautiful cardboard star rips in half. Ella and Olivia are each left holding a piece of the broken star.

'Oh no!' says Mum, 'I thought you were angels!'

'That's a terrible shame,' says Dad, sadly.

'I told you it should have been my turn,' grumbles Uncle Stu.

Ella and Olivia feel bad for ruining the star. That night, a little bit of the fun has been taken out of Christmas. But both girls secretly know it was their turn to put the gold star on the tree.

Chapter Two

No-one can remember
whose turn it was to put up
the star this year. Uncle Stu
taped it up before he went
home, but it still doesn't
look right. Even perched at
the top of the tree,
Ella and Olivia
can both see the
sticky tape.

'I'm sorry,' Ella says.

'Me too,' says Olivia.

But the damage is done.

'You girls must be on your best behaviour before Christmas,' Mum reminds both of them.

'Bluurrghhh,' agrees Max.

'Presents only come to well-behaved children,' Dad says. He has some presents to put under the Christmas tree.

The tags say, 'for Olivia', 'for Ella' and 'for Max'.
'Can we open our presents now?' asks Ella.

Christmas is still DAYS away.
'Don't touch these, girls!'
Dad warns. 'They are from
your Aunty Anne and Uncle
John. They arrived early. If
you open them . . .'
'WE WON'T!' cries Olivia.
Why would she want to ruin
the surprise before Christmas
Day? But Ella wants to open
her present straight away.
She can't possibly wait until
Christmas!

For a moment, the girls forget about the broken star.

There is a big red parcel in the shape of a box for Ella. There is a long, odd-shaped green parcel for Olivia. Max's gift is buried somewhere under the pile of presents.

Bob is curious about
the new tree. He sniffs
the trunk. He paws the
decorations. He barks at
the Christmas lights.
Flash, flash, flash,
go the lights.
'Woof, woof, woof,' goes
Bob.
Bob loves the smell of
the tree in the air and
the crinkly sound of the
wrapping paper around
all the presents.

'No, Bob!' says Ella. 'The presents aren't for you!' Bob ignores her. He just scampers around like it's already Christmas.

'I hope I get some Cool Kitties!' says Olivia.

Ella wants a new netball so that she can practise her shooting during summer. She was goal shooter last season. Next season she wants to score even more goals. Apart from the netball, she would like some colouring pencils, a scooter, some cool bracelets and a kitten.

'Miss Sparkle also needs some new clothes,' says Olivia. 'She needs a purple dress and some new shoes.' Olivia also wants a super-shooter water gun, a skipping rope and a bike.

On their way to bed that night, Ella tells Olivia a secret.

'I want to open my present from Aunty Anne and Uncle John,' she whispers.

'NO!' says Olivia. 'We will get into trouble again!'

'It can't hurt to open just one present before Christmas,' whispers Ella. She is SURE that no-one will find out.

'I don't know . . .' says Olivia.

'Good night, girls,' says Dad.

Those girls are up to something! he thinks.

Ella and Olivia fall asleep with butterflies in their tummies. It couldn't hurt to take a peek at their presents . . . could it?

Chapter Three

Christmas is only a day away. The house is getting very busy!

Ella and Olivia are finally on school holidays. They pack their uniforms away for the summer. Their schoolbags go into the cupboard until the first day back next year.

'Where are my magical elves?' asks Dad. He needs Ella and Olivia's help around the house.

First, they hang the stockings on the mantelpiece. There is a little one for Max, a medium one for Olivia and a large one for Ella.

'That's not fair!' says Olivia. 'Ella has more room for presents in her stocking!'

'The oldest always gets the most presents,' says Ella. 'That's not true,' says Dad. 'Everyone gets the same amount. And you three are very lucky. You probably get more things than anyone else in the neighbourhood!'

Dad and the girls continue with all the odd jobs. Ella and Olivia want to help, to make up for breaking the Christmas star.

They help Dad make the beds for Nanna and Grandad. They dust the spare room and throw open the windows. Ella leaves her favourite purple torch on Nanna's bedside table, just in case she needs it.

Later, the girls help Mum make some treats for Christmas Day. There are cakes to be decorated, and cutlery to be polished.

'You're being very helpful today, girls,' says Mum. She is pleased that Ella and Olivia are helping out today.

Everyone is looking forward to Christmas. Mum plays some Christmas carols very LOUDLY and Dad sings along in a silly voice.

Ella and Olivia decorate the Christmas cupcakes. Ella puts the icing on and Olivia lines them up neatly. The icing is red and green, and Ella makes swirls on the top of the cakes.

'Let's open one of our presents tonight,' Ella says very quietly.
'How will we wrap them back up?' whispers Olivia.

'We'll have to be very careful,' Ella says.
'Do you think we will see Santa?' Olivia asks.
'I hope so!' Ella answers.

'What are you two whispering about?' Dad asks. 'Are you up to no good?'

'Nothing, Dad,' the girls say. And they smile very sweetly. Dad frowns. Now he KNOWS they are keeping a secret.

Bob runs madly around the kitchen.

'NO, Bob!' says Mum. She shoos him out of the kitchen. It is no place for a puppy! 'It's time to take Bob for a walk,' Dad says, 'once you've finished those cupcakes.'

Bob loves going for a walk. He sniffs the breeze. He barks at other dogs. There are Christmas lights in all the yards: in trees and bushes, on porches and fences, and even on roofs!

All the jobs are finished by the time Nanna and Grandad arrive. Everything is ready for Christmas! Ella and Olivia are bursting inside. Christmas is only a day away . . . and tonight they will check their presents!

Chapter Four

It is the night before Christmas. Not a creature is stirring, except for Bob. 'He knows something exciting is about to happen,' says Dad.

Everyone squeezes on the couch to read *'Twas the Night Before Christmas*. Including Bob. He sits on Ella's lap and watches as they turn the pages.

'And to all a good night,' Mum reads. That is the end of the story!

Finally, it is time for bed. Ella carefully chops up some carrots for Santa's reindeer. She scatters them outside. 'What about Santa?' Dad asks. Olivia prepares a snack for Santa. He must get tired! She pours him a tall glass of milk and puts some of their cupcakes on a plate.

'Good job,' says Dad. Ella
and Olivia are so excited.
The plan is to wake up in
the middle of the night and
check on their presents.
They might even see Santa.
Before they get into bed,
Ella reminds Olivia of their
secret plan.
'Don't forget,' she whispers.
'Tonight is the night!'

Brrinnngg! goes Ella's alarm.

'Wake up, Olivia,' whispers Ella. The house is very quiet. Ella and Olivia stop at Mum and Dad's door on their way to the Christmas tree. They are both snoring very loudly. It is safe to go and check the Christmas presents! The girls tiptoe to the lounge room. They avoid the squeaky floorboard and push open the door.

There is not a sound. The Christmas tree lights glow softly. Ella can see their presents on the top of the pile.

'Quick, Olivia!' she cries. 'Let's look!'

Ella sneaks over to the tree. Just as the girls are about to open their presents, they hear a noise. Someone is coming!

'Olivia!' cries Ella. 'Hide!' She grabs Olivia's hand and they dive under the dining table. Just as they squeeze underneath, the lounge room door swings open.

'Uh-oh,' whispers Olivia.

'Shhhhhhhh!' cries Ella. 'Someone might hear us!' They hear heavy footsteps. Someone is in the lounge room. Someone with big, noisy shoes. The footsteps get louder, and then they stop.

From under the table, Ella and Olivia see big, black boots standing near them. They hold their breath and hope that they aren't discovered.

The boots then walk across the room to the Christmas tree. PHEW! The girls can hear the pounding of their own hearts. Olivia clutches Ella's hand.

There is the sound of
rustling, and the scrape of
a chair. Could it really be
Santa in their lounge room?
Olivia shuts her eyes tight.
She doesn't want to get into
trouble from Mum or Dad.
Or Santa!

Then the big, black boots walk past the table again and out of the room. There is not a sound, apart from the ticking of the grandfather clock in the room. The girls are finally alone again.

'We'll count to ten,' says Ella, 'and then see if the coast is clear.' Olivia nods. In the dark, the girls count slowly to ten.

Olivia still has her eyes closed. When she opens them, she can't believe what she sees! There are more presents under the tree. She can't even see the ones from Aunty Anne and Uncle John!

'The cakes are gone!' Ella whispers. There are only crumbs left on the plate, and the glass of milk is empty.

'The stockings are full,' whispers Olivia.

'Let's go,' says Ella. She takes her sister's hand. 'We really should be in bed!'

The two girls snuggle under their covers. Their hearts are still pounding. They fall asleep straight away, with visions of wrapped presents dancing in their heads.

Chapter Five

Brrinnngg! Ella doesn't hear her alarm for the second time on Christmas morning. Mum and Dad are puzzled. Usually, Ella and Olivia are awake at the crack of dawn. Instead, Max wakes up first. He can't wait for his presents!

When they finally wake up,
both girls stay in their beds.
Was it all a dream or did
they really see Santa?

Soon enough, they are up
and jumping on Mum
and Dad's bed.

They just have to know if
what they saw was real.
'Wake up!' cries Olivia.
'Merry Christmas!'
'Did we dream it all?' Ella
whispers to Olivia.

Everyone sleepily heads into the lounge room. Nanna and Grandad are still rubbing their eyes. They are not usually up this early!

When Olivia and Ella see the tree, they know they have not been dreaming. There is no spare space at all under there! There are so many presents for everyone: for Max, for Mum and Dad, for Nanna and Grandad.

There is even a present
under the tree for Bob!

'Wow,' says Dad softly.
'Amazing,' says Mum.
'Santa has definitely been
here!' Olivia cries.
But she can't say too much
more. It might give their
secret away.

Together, in the daylight,
the girls check the room for
more signs of Santa.

'The milk and cakes
are gone, too,' Ella tells
everyone. 'There are only
crumbs on the plate we left
out for him.'

Ella and Olivia rush to the
back door. All the carrots
have disappeared.
'The reindeer must have
eaten them!' says Olivia.

'And look!' says Ella. Everyone turns to look at the Christmas tree. A beautiful new gold star sits perfectly on top of the tree.

'Do you think Santa found our house?' asks Dad.

'OF COURSE,' say the girls. There is so much more that they want to say! They weren't supposed to be awake in the middle of the night. They weren't allowed to be snooping around the presents before Christmas Day. And they definitely weren't planning on seeing Santa!

'Girls,' Mum says. 'I think you missed something . . .'

There, in the corner of the room, is a brand-new bike with a bow. 'For Olivia, from Santa' it says on the tag. Next to it is a brand-new scooter, with tinsel hanging from the handlebars.

'For Ella, from Santa' the card reads.

The two girls look at each other. How did Santa know exactly what they wanted? And why didn't they see them last night?

'I didn't see . . .' says Olivia.
'See what?' asks Mum. Then
Olivia stops.
'Nothing, Mum,' the girls say.
'I'm so glad we didn't open
our presents,' Ella whispers
to Olivia.
'Me too!' agrees Olivia.

Both girls share a secret
smile. Ella and Olivia got
something even better than
presents . . . a real Christmas
surprise!

COLLECT THEM ALL!

To find out more go to: EllaandOlivia.com.a where you can play games and do more fun stuff!